Little Elephant Thunderfoot

For the teachers and pupils
of the Richard Pate School

Dedicated to the work of Elefriends
S. G.

For Louise
J. B.

ORCHARD BOOKS
338 Euston Road, London NW1 3BH
Orchard Books Australia
Level 17/207 Kent Street, Sydney, NSW 2000

First published in 1996 by Orchard Books
First published in paperback in 1998
This edition published in 2009

ISBN 978 1 40830 086 2

Text © Sally Grindley 1996
Illustrations © John Butler 1996
The right of Sally Grindley to be identified as the author and of John Butler to identified as the illustrator
of this work has been asserted by them in accordance with the Copyright, Designs and Patents Act, 1988.
A CIP catalogue record for this book is available from the British Library.

1 3 5 7 9 10 8 6 4 2

Printed in China

Orchard Books is a division of Hachette Children's Books, an Hachette Livre UK company.
www.hachettelivre.co.uk

Little Elephant
Thunderfoot

Sally Grindley

John Butler

ORCHARD BOOKS

Little Elephant was only twenty minutes old
but he knew he had to stand up. With one
almighty effort, he gathered all four baggy
grey legs beneath him and pushed. His head
popped up above the undergrowth.

One more push and he was standing.
He rocked unsteadily in the breeze.

Sundance, Little Elephant's mother, stood close by and guided him to her milk. He sucked hungrily, while Sundance ran her trunk gently over her son's body. Little Elephant felt warm and safe as he learned his mother's taste and smell.

Wise Old One was Little Elephant's
grandmother and the head of the herd.
She had roamed the Savannah for fifty
years. She was the eyes, the ears, and
the trunk of the family. She showed
them where to feed and where to play.
She showed them where there was water,
and what to do when danger was near.

Little Elephant was scared of his
grandmother at first, because she looked
so enormous. But he soon learned that
Wise Old One was a gentle giant, and
then he loved to be close to her.

As Little Elephant grew stronger, he began to leave his mother's side. He played with his sisters, chasing through the long elephant grass. They gambolled along with wobbly heads and floppy trunks, kicking their legs out behind them, just for the fun of it.

Wise Old One called him Little Thunderfoot because he made so much noise.

It was a while before Little Thunderfoot knew what his trunk was for.
It seemed to wave around in front of his face without him doing anything.
Then Wise Old One showed him how to touch and feel with it, and Little
Thunderfoot liked putting the end in his mouth to try out different tastes.

Sometimes, he would playfully pull his grandmother's tail with his trunk
and she would butt him with her head.

Little Thunderfoot liked it best when Wise Old One led the family to the river. The elephants would rush into the water and wriggle and wrestle and splash.

Little Thunderfoot even dared to squirt Wise Old One with water and his grandmother sprayed him back.

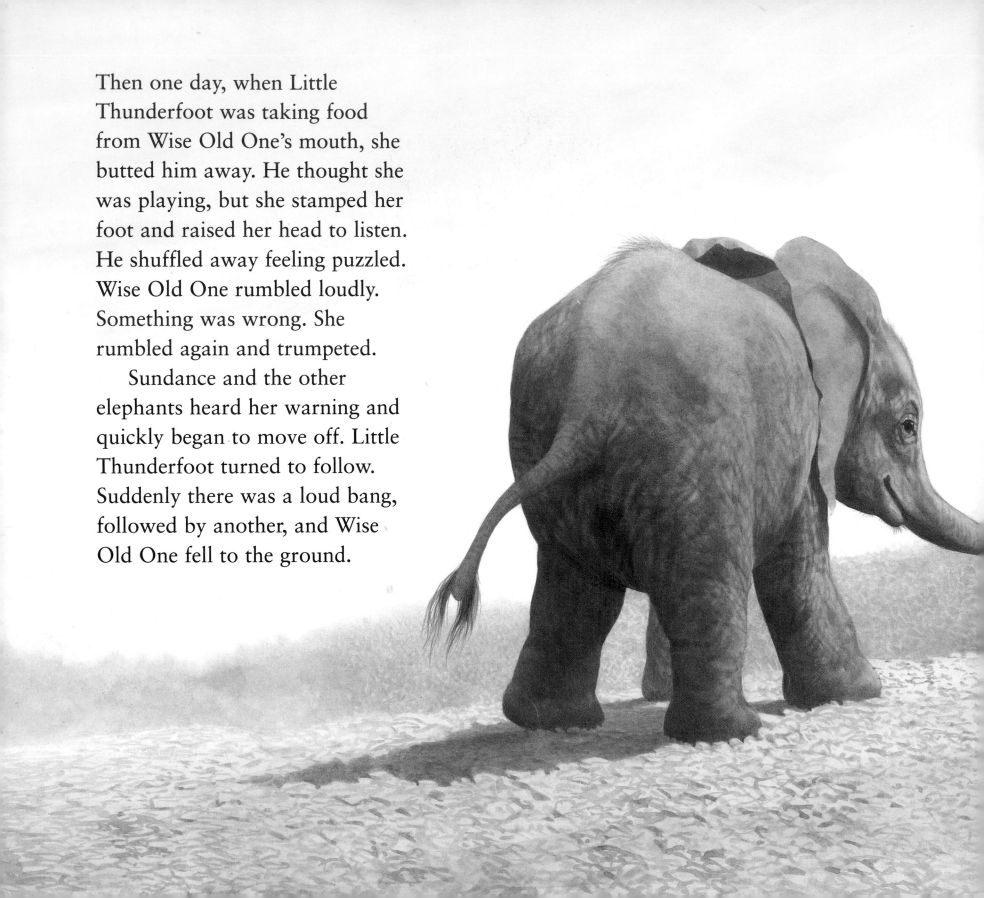

Then one day, when Little
Thunderfoot was taking food
from Wise Old One's mouth, she
butted him away. He thought she
was playing, but she stamped her
foot and raised her head to listen.
He shuffled away feeling puzzled.
Wise Old One rumbled loudly.
Something was wrong. She
rumbled again and trumpeted.

Sundance and the other
elephants heard her warning and
quickly began to move off. Little
Thunderfoot turned to follow.
Suddenly there was a loud bang,
followed by another, and Wise
Old One fell to the ground.

The elephants saw Wise
Old One fall and stampeded.
Little Thunderfoot stared at
his grandmother and waited
for her to stand up and go
with them, but she didn't
move. He went back and
touched her with his trunk,
but still Wise Old One
didn't move.

Little Thunderfoot turned in fear and ran after his family. They ran and ran, not really knowing where except that they had to get away. At last they found a safe place where dense thickets would protect them from danger.

They pressed close together and touched each others faces. They entwined trunks and rumbled and wheezed. They shook their heads and scraped the ground.

Frightened and confused, Little Thunderfoot pushed against Sundance for comfort. She stroked him with her trunk, but Little Thunderfoot sensed her panic. When would Wise Old One come and show them what to do?

When dawn broke, Sundance
led her family back to where
her mother still lay. She began
to explore and caress every inch
of Wise Old One's body with
her trunk. Little Thunderfoot
joined in with the other elephants
and felt the sadness overcome
them. His grandmother wasn't
coming back.

They touched Wise Old One
one last time, then Sundance
began to rip up clumps of grass
and earth and throw them over
her. Little Thunderfoot helped
as best he could, he wanted his
grandmother to be safe. It took
all morning to cover her up.

Then Sundance led her family away. The elephants moved quickly, heading for the hills. Little Thunderfoot found it hard to keep up as he was still just a baby.

They walked and walked for several days and nights. From time to time they stopped to listen and smell, their trunks held high to test the breeze. Little Thunderfoot grew tired and very hungry.

Then in the distance they saw another group of elephants.

Little Thunderfoot felt his mother's excitement push her sadness
away for a brief moment. Sundance trumpeted loudly and charged
triumphantly over to the group. With a great clacking of tusks,
she greeted Moonwalk and then buried her head in her sister's side.
Little Thunderfoot moved between them. Now he felt safe again.

Sundance and Moonwalk and their families stayed together. It was not easy for them without Wise Old One because she knew so much. But they helped each other along and as time passed each day became a little easier.

There were play times again, and bath times and fun times. But Little Thunderfoot would never forget his grandmother.

 # Elefacts

Elephants are the largest land mammals. They are immensely
strong, very intelligent, peaceful and fun-loving.
They can live for up to seventy years.

A pregnant elephant carries her baby for nearly two years.
As soon as the calf is born, it will stand up and begin
to feed on its mother's milk.

The oldest female leads the herd, which will normally be made up
of daughters and granddaughters, as well as sisters and their
offspring. They all help to look after the youngest elephants.
The males grow up within the herd, but leave to live on their own
when they are about sixteen years old.

When a member of the herd dies, the other elephants often cover
the body and mourn. An elephant's only enemy is man.

To find out more about the conservation and protection of elephants, and a
unique elephant adoption scheme, contact: ELEFRIENDS/THE BORN FREE FOUNDATION,
Coldharbour, Dorking, Surrey RH5 6HA

(Registered charity no. 296024)